Ludlow Laughs

ha ha ha ha

by Jon Agee

A Sunburst Book
Farrar Straus Giroux

dedicated to the memory of
Woody J. Baumhacker

Copyright © 1985 by Jon Agee • All rights reserved
Library of Congress catalog card number: 85-45466
Distributed in Canada by Douglas & McIntyre Ltd.
Printed in Singapore • First edition, 1985
Sunburst edition, 1987 • 14 13 12 11 10 9 8 7 6 5

When Ludlow was born,
everyone immediately noticed
this shape:

It wasn't a cute little dimple.
It wasn't an adorable nose.

And as the rest of him grew
and developed
and changed

IT DIDN'T.
It only
opened for food,
an occasional *Burp!*
and plenty of grumbling.

Ludlow
worked in a
complaint
department.

At the end of the day,
he felt grumpier than ever.

Night after night he came home,
grumbling and growling,
and went to bed.
But one night something happened.

Ludlow had a dream.
Not just any dream—
THE FUNNIEST DREAM IN THE WORLD!!!

He giggled. He guffawed.
And he laughed in his sleep loud enough
for the whole neighborhood to hear.

Nobody had ever heard laughing like that before. What was even stranger was that once they heard it they couldn't help laughing themselves!

The morning
was the usual routine,
grumbling all the way to work,
grumbling all the way home.

But that night it happened again!
Ludlow's dream was even *funnier*!
Now the whole *town* was laughing.

If a whole town
could laugh with Ludlow,
why not the whole *country*?
A local radio station was
interested in the
possibilities.

Very quietly they hooked up their equipment.

Suddenly Ludlow
was on the air!

Soon the whole *world* was laughing with Ludlow.

Ho HO HO
Heh Heh Heh Heh Heh Heh Heh
Huh Huh Huh Huh H
HA HA HA HA
he he he he
ha ha ha ha ha
hee haw
hee hee
ha ha ha
ho ho ho
har har har
ho

When morning came, the radio crew
packed up their things and crept away.
Ludlow woke up—his old self again.

And so it went, night after night,
for months on end, until one night
the world was quiet.
Something was wrong.
Ludlow wasn't laughing!!!
What could they do?
The radio crew was desperate.

Outside, the world was growing restless.
From South Pole to North Pole there
was no Ludlow on the radio.

Nothing the radio crew did made
Ludlow laugh. So they packed up their
equipment and left.

All through the night Ludlow slept, quietly.
And when he woke up, something had changed.